Little Dragonfly's Quilt

Alaska Animals Solve a Color Puzzle

D. Katharine Adams

illustrated by
Beth Pennington Taylor

Publication Consultants

Since 1978

PO Box 221974 Anchorage, Alaska 99522-1974
Books@publicationconsultants.com — www.publicationconsultants.com

ISBN 978-1-59433-045-2

Library of Congress Catalog Card Number: 2006903546

Copyright 2006 by D. Katharine Adams
—First Edition—

Printed in China

Author's Note

Alaska's official insect is the dragonfly. The Four-spotted Skimmer dragonfly (*Libellula quadrimaculata*) was chosen in 1995, after the students of the Auntie Mary Nicoli Elementary School in Aniak campaigned on its behalf during a statewide contest. The dragonfly won the contest with 3,914 votes compared to 3,035 votes for the mosquito!

• Aniak

Dedication and Acknowledgements

For my children, Merrick and Oliver, with love. And for Mary A. Nordale, with affection and gratitude. You truly exemplify Helen Adams Keller's words: "I can not do everything, but I can do something. I must not fail to do the something that I can do." Thank you for "doing something."

D. Katharine Adams

To my children Heidi, Jodi, and Read with love. Thank you for teaching me how to 'buck up.' In memory of my mother, Gladys Tyson Pennington, who instilled and encouraged creativity in all aspects of my life. Thank you for all the crayons and paper—as far back as I can remember.

Beth Pennington Taylor

3

Little Dragonfly flitted through the meadow wildflowers, the sun shimmering on her wings. "Three weeks until Mother's birthday, how exciting!" thought Little Dragonfly. "Darling Mother deserves the nicest present in the whole world."

"It should be beautiful, warm,
and friendly, just like Mother.
Flowers? Nectar? Bright bubble balloons?
I know," said Little Dragonfly, "a quilt!"

6

"But what color should it be?" wondered Little Dragonfly. She thought of all the iridescent colors of dragonflies, butterflies, and hummingbirds that lived in the woodlands.

"I'll ask Hummingbird," she said.

7

Little Dragonfly found Hummingbird gathering nectar
in a Sitka rosebush near the edge of the meadow.
"What is your favorite color, Hummingbird?" asked Little Dragonfly.

"I love the luscious red of the Sitka rose that
gives me the sweetest nectar," said Hummingbird.
"My favorite color is red."

8

So Little Dragonfly decided to make a red quilt.

Butterfly fluttered
onto a nearby Icelandic Poppy.
"What is your favorite color,
Butterfly?" asked Little Dragonfly.
"I love the bright orange of the
Icelandic Poppy. It is the same
color as my wings," said Butterfly.

"My favorite color is orange."

So Little Dragonfly decided to make
a red and orange quilt.

Just then Bunny came bouncing by with a bunch of buttercups.
"What is your favorite color, Bunny?" asked Little Dragonfly.
"I love the golden yellow of buttercups," said Bunny,
"it reminds me of the warm sun."

"My favorite color is yellow."

So Little Dragonfly decided to make
a red and orange and yellow quilt.

Flying over the tundra on her way home,
Little Dragonfly spied Tundra Swan.
"What is your favorite color, Tundra Swan?"

14

"I love the soft green of the springtime tundra where I lay my eggs," said Tundra Swan.

"My favorite color is green."

So Little Dragonfly decided to make
a red and orange and yellow and green quilt.

15

But as she passed the blueberry bushes
Little Dragonfly saw Baby Bear.

"What is your favorite color, Baby Bear?"

"I love the blue of blueberries sparkling with dew that I gobble up for breakfast," said Baby Bear. "My favorite color is blue."

So Little Dragonfly decided to make a red and orange and yellow and green and blue quilt.

17

Continuing on her way home, Little Dragonfly
caught sight of Caribou drinking from a creek.
A cluster of purpley-blue wild iris just beginning
to bloom made a carpet next to the creek.

"What is your favorite color, Caribou?"
asked Little Dragonfly.

"I love purpley-blue indigo.
It is just the indigo color
of the wild iris that bloom
next to the creek," said Caribou.

"My favorite color is indigo."

So Little Dragonfly decided to make
a red and orange and yellow and green
and blue and indigo quilt.

Very close to home now, Little Dragonfly
had visions of the fine quilt she would make.
"I love the color of the very fragrant violets that
grow next to my home in the bog," said Little Dragonfly.

"Violet is just the color of Mother's gorgeous wings!"
exclaimed Little Dragonfly. "My favorite color is violet."

So Little Dragonfly decided to make
a red and orange and yellow and green
and blue and indigo and violet quilt.

Home at last!

Little Dragonfly set about making a lovely quilt.
She used delicate stitches to piece together the
radiant colors. She sewed and sewed and sewed.

Tomorrow was Mother's birthday and at last the quilt
was complete. Little Dragonfly carefully washed and
then hung the finished quilt out in the garden to dry.

24

But that night, a wild storm blew in
and knocked the precious quilt to the ground.
In the morning, Little Dragonfly wept
to see her gift so wet and bedraggled.

As the sun rose in the sky,
Little Dragonfly picked up the
quilt and shook it out to dry.
A playful gust of wind caught
the quilt and lifted it into the air.

The quilt floated higher and higher,
billowing up into a beautiful arch.

27

And to this day when you see a rainbow, you will know

that a dragonfly has spread out her quilt to dry!

Dragonfly Facts

With the sun flashing on their shimmering wings, it is easy to see why dragonflies have inspired such lovely names as Angel Wings, Golden Rings, and River Emeralds.

Don't be deceived by their beauty. Dragonflies, sometimes called mosquito hawks, devour billions of mosquitoes each year. They also eat flies, gnats and other flying insects.

More than 5,000 different species (kinds) of dragonflies exist throughout the world. They are found on every continent except Antarctica. The scientific name for this large group of insects is Odonata. "Odon" is the Greek word for tooth. Dragonflies use their teeth to catch and eat all those mosquitoes.

Dragonflies have been both feared and admired. In most European countries they once were called names such as "devil's darning needle" and "horse-stingers." Dragonflies, however, do not have stingers and can't hurt people or animals. In ancient Japan the dragonfly was believed to bring good luck in battle. According to legend,

Japan was once known as Akitsu-shimu which means Dragonfly Island.

Dragonflies are able to catch their meals easily because their wings allow them to fly forward and backward and turn quickly. Just like a helicopter, they can take off straight up and hover almost without moving for long periods at a time. They have excellent eyesight, among the best of all insects. A dragonfly can see in front, left and right, above and below; and with only a slight turn of its head, it can see behind, too.

A 325-million-year-old dragonfly fossil discovered in Germany had a wingspan of 27 inches! Other fossils of ancient giant dragonflies have been found in France and in Kansas.

Dragonflies are helpful to people because they eat so many mosquitoes and some mosquitoes carry diseases such as malaria. But these shy creatures (some dragonflies are so shy that they "play dead" if frightened) need clean water to survive. We can help protect these beautiful and useful creatures by cleaning up polluted rivers and lakes and saving their wetland habitats.

ODONATA

Do you see her

Radiant beauty?

Angel Wings, Golden Rings, Jewels, and River Emeralds.

Glamorous, but deadly to her prey,

Odonata is her name.

Not harmful to people, animals, or plants; this

Fascinating insect catches mosquitoes in flight. She

Lived long before dinosaurs, for more than 100 million years.

Yes, she is a treasure.

Sun shimmering on flashing wings, this Dragonfly, Odonata!

GLOSSARY

Arch (arch) *noun* A curved structure.

Bedraggled (bi – drag – uhld) *adjective* Wet, limp, or soiled; messy.

Billowing (bil – oh – ing) *verb* Pushed outward by the wind.

Dew (doo) *noun* Water in the form of small drops that collects overnight on cool surfaces outside.

Flit (flit) *verb* To move lightly and swiftly; fly, dart, or skim along.

Flutter (fluht – ur) *verb* To wave or flap rapidly.

Fragrant (fray – gruhnt) *adjective* Having a sweet smell.

Gust (guhst) *noun* A sudden, strong blast of wind.

Indigo (in – duh – go) *noun* A dark violet-blue color or dye.

Iridescent (ir – i – des – uhnt) *adjective* A display of lustrous, rainbow-like colors.

Luscious (luhsh – uhss) *adjective* Delicious.

Nectar (nek – tur) *noun* A sweet liquid that bees collect from flowers and turn into honey.

Radiant (ray -dee – uhnt) *adjective* Bright and shining.

Shimmering (shim – ur – ing) *verb* Shining with a faint, unsteady light.

Tundra (tuhn – druh) *noun* A flat and treeless arctic region.

Wept (wept) *verb* To cry.

Sources: Scholastic Children's Dictionary, Revised Edition, 1996; Webster's New Universal Unabridged Dictionary, 2003; and the on-line dictionary Wiktionary.